PUFFIN BOOKS
Mice and Mendelson

'A piano? Why, in the name of Shadrach, Meshach and Abednego, should I get your pony a piano?' asked the Old Lord.

'Mr Mendelson likes thinking about tunes,' said Sam.

'But he can't *play* a piano.'

'No,' said Sam. 'But his friends Bertha and Gertrude can.'

Bertha and Gertrude were not horses, they were field-mice. Every night, on the dot of six o'clock, they would have a concert of piano music especially for Mr Mendelson. Side by side on the keyboard, dashing to and fro, they would play the most beautiful waltzes and polkas, mazurkas and minuets, while Mr Mendelson stood breathing heavily with pleasure, gazing in wonder and admiration at his clever friends.

All would have been well, and the time before Sam came back from school would have passed peacefully, had it not been for the evil schemes of sneaky Dan Sligo. Trickery, deception and theft were second nature to him, and cheating the simple old pony out of his piano should have been easy. Except that Dan kept forgetting Bertha and Gertrude, who did their best to thwart him at every turn.

Joan Aiken tickles the imagination with her lovable Mr Mendelson and the quick-witted mice in their hilarious efforts to defeat the dastardly Dan Sligo.

D1147488

Joan Aiken

Mice
and
Mendelson

Illustrated by Babette Cole

Music by
John Sebastian Brown

PUFFIN BOOKS

Puffin Books, Penguin Books Ltd, Harmondsworth, Middlesex, England
Penguin Books, 625 Madison Avenue, New York, New York 10022, U.S.A.
Penguin Books Australia Ltd, Ringwood, Victoria, Australia
Penguin Books Canada Ltd, 2801 John Street, Markham, Ontario, Canada L3R 1B4
Penguin Books (N.Z.) Ltd, 182–190 Wairau Road, Auckland 10, New Zealand

These stories were first transmitted in 1977
by Thames Television in a series produced and
directed by Peter Webb

First published by Jonathan Cape 1978
Published in Puffin Books 1981

Made and printed in Great Britain by
Richard Clay (The Chaucer Press) Ltd,
Bungay, Suffolk
Set in Monotype Baskerville

Contents

Two Mice and Mendelson

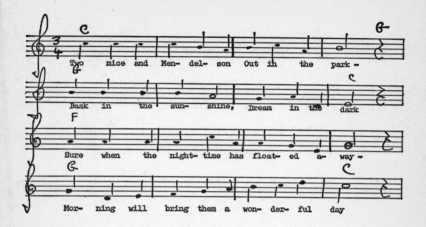

Two mice and Mendelson, out in the park
    Bask in the sunshine, dream in the dark
Sure when the night time has floated away
Morning will bring them a wonderful day.

Two mice and Mendelson, out in the park
    Frolic in sunshine, doze in the dark
Listen to rain, sniff the wind when it blows –
What they don't know about, nobody knows.

The Bag of Time

Far to the north of England there is a big wild neglected park, known as Midnight Park. In this park, about a hundred years ago, lived an aged Orkney pony whose name was Mr Mendelson. He was only about three feet high – if he had been standing on the other side of a kitchen table, all you could have seen would have been

his head. But his head was big and handsome, so that he looked like a much larger horse, whose legs were only half the proper length. He was black all over, except for one white triangular patch in the middle of his back, which was covered by a saddle when he wore one. His coat was very thick and shaggy, and his tail was so long that it almost touched the ground. This was very convenient for his friends Gertrude and Bertha. I will come to them presently.

Mr Mendelson had been ridden for years by a boy called Sam. But the day came at last when Sam grew too big for the old pony, and his legs touched the ground on either side. And very soon after that, Sam had to go away to boarding-school.

'Old Mr Mendelson is going to be lonely when I'm gone,' Sam said to his grandfather, who was called the Old Lord. (Sam's mother and father had died.)

'Perhaps I ought to sell him to someone who will ride him?' said the Old Lord doubtfully, putting a plate of porridge in front of Sam.

Sam and his grandfather were having breakfast in the stable, where they lived. (The big house in the middle of the park had burned down long ago.) The Old Lord was in a wheelchair, because he had rheumatism, which made him very lame. But he could get about in his wheelchair much faster than most people can walk. He always made the breakfast. Sam washed up afterwards.

'No, *no*,' said Sam. 'I didn't mean we should *sell* Mr Mendelson. What I meant was that you should get him a piano.'

'A piano? Why, in the name of Shadrach, Meshach and Abednego, should I get him a piano?'

'He likes thinking about tunes,' said Sam.

'But he can't *play* a piano.'

'No,' said Sam. 'But his friends Bertha and Gertrude can.'

Gertrude and Bertha were not horses. I will come to them in a minute.

'There's the old piano you gave to the town band,' Sam went on. 'Now there's no town band, nobody uses it. You could have that put in the park, under the big oak.'

'Oh, very well!' said the Old Lord. 'And I suppose you'll want it covered with a tarpaulin to keep off the rain?'

'Yes,' said Sam.

Then the carriage came to take Sam to the train

which was to take him to boarding-school. So he rubbed
Mr Mendelson's nose for the last time, said good-bye to
his grandfather, and got into the carriage, and it drove
away.

The Old Lord had the piano moved into the park.

'There!' he said to Mr Mendelson. 'That's for you
and your friends.'

And he rolled himself back to the stable in his
wheelchair.

Mr Mendelson, of course, could not play the piano.
But his friends Bertha and Gertrude could play remark-
ably well.

Gertrude and Bertha were fieldmice. At one time a musician had lived in the old ice-house in a corner of the park. They had learned to play from watching him. So they were delighted when Mr Mendelson's piano was put under the big oak.

'Every night we'll play tunes to you,' said Gertrude.

'Why not every day?' said Mr Mendelson.

'We have our mousework to do in the daytime,' said Bertha.

The two mice kept tremendously busy all day, sweeping and dusting. One of their biggest jobs was tidying Mr Mendelson. This took hours, for his coat

was so thick that it held any amount of dust. They had to go all over him inch by inch, brushing and beating with bunches of twigs, raking and scraping and currying with their tiny comb-like claws, so that he always had a beautiful shine on his thick black coat; and they also combed and teased out his long black mane and tail (in which there were now some white hairs) until each hair hung separate and shining. In return for this kindness, Mr Mendelson allowed them to take as much hair and fluff as they wished for a warm lining for their nest. And he also carried them about the park, and allowed them to use him as a step-ladder to reach fruit and nuts on the high blackberry clumps and hazel-bushes in the park. Which saved them a great deal of trouble and climbing.

'We'll have a concert of piano music every evening at six o'clock,' said Gertrude.

'Please!' said Mr Mendelson. 'Will you tell me how I am going to *know* when it's six o'clock? Suppose I am over on the other side of the park?'

'You can see the stable clock on its tower from any-where in the park,' said Bertha.

'But I can't tell the time!'

'When one hand points straight down, one hand points straight up, that's six o'clock.'

'All right,' said Mr Mendelson. 'That I can remember.'

So every day as he wandered about the park munching grass, he kept a careful eye on the stable clock.

And when one hand pointed down, and one up, he

would gallop to the piano from wherever he was and drag off the tarpaulin with his teeth.

Then the mice would run up Mr Mendelson's tail on to the keyboard, and, side by side, dashing to and fro, they would play the most beautiful waltzes and polkas, mazurkas and minuets, while Mr Mendelson stood breathing heavily with pleasure, gazing in wonder and admiration at his clever friends, with his chin resting on the end of the keyboard, so that the vibrations from the music went right down his neck to his tail.

And all day, as he wandered about the park, the beautiful tunes danced inside his head.

At first, sometimes, there was a little trouble about the *time*.

'So why aren't you playing?' Mr Mendelson would demand. 'It's six o'clock already, and I've taken off the tarpaulin. Leave combing my tail and play the music, please, ladies!'

'It isn't six o'clock yet, Mr Mendelson. It's only half-past twelve.'

'But one of the hands points up, and one is down.'

'The *small* hand has to be *up*, and the *large* hand has to be *down*.'

'Large hand, small hand!' grumbled Mr Mendelson. 'Why do they have to make time so complicated, answer me that?'

Then the winter evenings came, and it was dark by teatime.

'Now I can't see the stable clock at all! So what am I supposed to do, wait till the moon rises? By then it will be too late, probably!'

'You must listen till you hear the stable clock strike six,' said Bertha.

'How do I know what is six?'

'One strike for each foot,' said Gertrude, running up and down his legs.

'And one for each ear,' said Bertha, biting them affectionately.

'Four and two makes six!'

'Do me a favour! I'm too old to learn all this complicated mathematics!'

But just the same, Mr Mendelson did learn, and the only trouble then was that he would sometimes wake them in the middle of the night, shouting,

'Oy, ladies! Wake up! I heard the stable clock strike six – we must have been sleeping all day!'

'This is six o'clock in the *morning*, Mr Mendelson. Our concerts take place at six o'clock in the *evening*.'

'Oigh, may the devil fly away with them, why do they have to have *two* six o'clocks, will you tell me? Isn't there enough confusion already? Are they so stingy they couldn't afford another number?'

'Oh, never mind!' said Gertrude. 'We'll just *tell* you when it's time for the concert, Mr Mendelson. Then you won't have to waste your time worrying about it.'

'But I enjoy worrying! It doesn't waste any time at all!'

Meanwhile the two mice were becoming so expert on the piano that the Old Lord rolled himself over in his wheelchair almost every evening to listen to them.

Now there was also, at the time I am telling you about, a gipsy called Dan Sligo, who lived in the woods outside Midnight Park. He made a living from buying things cheaply off people who didn't realize they were being swindled, and then selling the things again at much higher prices to other people. Dan Sligo was also a thief, when he could steal without getting caught, and he had an uncommonly sharp eye for picking things up – he could spot a threepenny piece lying in a patch of dust that a hundred people had walked past without noticing.

When the piano was put out in the park for Mr Mendelson and his friends, Dan Sligo saw it, and he thought to himself,

'What a waste! Why should an old numbskull of a pony and two pernickety mice have a piano all to themselves?'

Which was not at all fair, for anybody who liked could come and listen to their music.

Dan Sligo set his wits to work, thinking how to get the piano away from them. It was no use trying to steal the piano under cover of dark, for Mr Mendelson was so fond of it that he stood sleeping all night with his chin resting on the keyboard. So presently Dan Sligo wandered along to Mr Mendelson, carrying a bag of fine grey ashes.

''Morning, Mr M!' said Dan. 'Not getting any younger, then, I see! White hair beginning to show in the old mane, eh?'

Bertha and Gertrude had just finished combing out Mr Mendelson's mane, and it hung all silky and black-and-white in the sunshine.

'What *you* need, Mr M,' said Dan Sligo, 'is a bag of time. Everybody needs more time as they get older. A few extra years'd come in handy, eh? And I've got the *very* thing for you, right here in my hand,' he said, dangling the bag of ashes under Mr Mendelson's nose.

'See here! This bag's plumb full, chock-a-block with time.'

'Time? Time?' murmured Mr Mendelson. 'Any more of that stuff, I don't need! Those mice give me plenty of trouble with time as it is.'

'O' *course* you need it!' said Dan Sligo. '*Everybody* needs more time. And here I've got a bag of it – real, vintage, 99 per cent proof, Grade-A, 22-carat, first-class time. It'd be worth its weight in diamonds if I could be bothered to take it to the Houses o' Parliament! Just look at that.'

He trickled a little dust out of the bag into the palm of his hand.

'See! That's ten minutes' worth. I'll make you a present of it. If you had the whole bag, Mr M, it'd give you days and weeks and months and years and centuries of extra time. Why – just think! you'd have two days to everybody else's one. When all the other folk was on to Thursday, you'd be having a second Wednesday!'

'Why would I be wanting two Wednesdays?' said Mr Mendelson, 'Enough is sufficient.'

'Humph,' said Dan Sligo. He saw that he must change his tactic a little. He said,

'How long do those mice play to you each evening?'

'A couple of hours.'

'Well! Just think – with this bag of time you could spread out that two hours to five or even six hours! And look – ' he went on, as Mr Mendelson still seemed doubtful, 'as we're pals, I'll throw in this handsome watch and chain, which you can wear round your neck. Then you won't have to worry about watching the stable clock – you'll be carrying your own time round with you.'

And Dan hung the watch round Mr Mendelson's

neck on its chain. It was a very old watch he had picked up in a spinney in the park. It was so corroded and caked with mud that it was quite black, and it had not gone for thirty years, but Mr Mendelson did not know that. He looked down at it rather proudly.

'See? You'll be the only horse in the north country wearing a watch. You'll wonder how you ever did without it – *or* this priceless bag of time,' said Dan, and he dropped the bag of ash between Mr Mendelson's feet. 'Now, the only thing I'll take in exchange – and I'm doing myself a bad turn, just because you're such a good friend, Mr M – is this old piano.'

Dan had already arranged to sell the piano for fifty

pounds to a pub called The King's Head. They needed a piano for a party that very night, and the landlord was waiting with a cart outside the park fence, ready to take it away. So Dan, who was very strong, pulled a rope from his pocket, knotted it round the piano once or twice, hoisted up the piano on to his back, and began to walk off with it.

Mr Mendelson gazed after him in stupefaction and horror.

'Oy! Hey! Wait!' he cried. 'You can't take the piano!'

'Sure, I can! I've given you a fine watch, and a bag of top quality time for it. Fair exchange is no robbery.'

Tears the size of golf balls began to roll down Mr Mendelson's nose.

'But how can we have our evening music if you take away our piano?'

'Go buy a harp!' called Dan Sligo mockingly.

However, just at that moment Bertha and Gertrude came bustling through the grass, and they saw the tears rolling down Mr Mendelson's nose. Bertha ran to wipe them up with a bunch of feathers, and Gertrude cried,

'Mr Mendelson, what's the matter? And why is Dan Sligo taking our piano?'

'I bought it from him at a fair price!' said Dan Sligo. 'I gave him a gentleman's half-hunter watch, and a bag of twenty-denier time.'

He was very annoyed that the mice had turned up, for he feared they would not be so easy to deal with as the old pony. And he was in a hurry, for the landlord of The King's Head had to be back at his pub by half-past five, and he had told Dan Sligo he must have the piano by a quarter-past five at the latest.

'You *must* let me play Mr Mendelson one last tune,' said Gertrude. 'See how upset he is! I'm sure he didn't understand that you were going to take the piano right away.'

'Of *course* he didn't,' said Bertha. 'You must let us each play a last tune. That's only fair.'

'Oh, very well,' said Dan. 'Only *one* tune each, though! I must take the piano by five o'clock.'

'All right,' said Bertha. 'We'll play till the stable clock says five. I'll go first,' she said, biting her sister's tail, 'and then it will be Gertrude's turn.'

So Dan Sligo irritably set the piano down again and

undid the knotted rope. He slapped open the lid, and Bertha ran up Mr Mendelson's tail on to the keyboard and started to play.

How she played! – with what agility and strength and brilliance, what runs and trills, what crashing chords, what spectacular leaps from black notes to white, and back to black again. It was more than a piece of piano music – it was a whole ballet as well. Even Dan Sligo was amazed. Some of the chords Bertha was obliged to play with her long tail, since her legs were too short to stretch. At last she was quite exhausted, and sank down panting on four white notes at the left-hand end of the piano – trrrump!

'Now I got to take the piano,' said Dan. 'I can see the landlord of The King's Head waiting.'

'No, no!' cried Gertrude. 'I haven't had my turn yet.' And before Dan Sligo could stop her, she too had scurried up Mr Mendelson's tail, and was dashing to and fro along the keyboard. Dan Sligo didn't like to shut down the lid on her, but he was very impatient.

'Come on, now, that's enough. That's quite enough!'

'No it's not, no it's not!' panted Gertrude, playing a magnificent arpeggio by dashing at top speed along half the length of the keyboard, pressing down the keys behind her with her tail. 'It isn't five o'clock yet!'

'It *must* be! You've been playing for at least an hour. I never heard such a long piece in my *life*.'

'Look at the stable clock,' said Bertha, who had her breath back by now. 'It only says half-past four.'

True enough it did, for while Bertha was playing,

Gertrude had scurried up inside the clock tower and wound a bit of wool round the pendulum, stopping the clock.

Dan looked over towards the park fence and saw that the landlord of The King's Head had whipped up his horse and was driving away to find himself another piano.

'The deal's off!' he shouted to Dan.

And then, since Gertrude was too tired to play any longer, Mr Mendelson said politely,

'I've been thinking, Mr Sligo, and I've decided I don't want your bag of time, *or* your watch, so you can take them back, thank you! I haven't used any of the time. And I would far rather keep my piano.'

'Oh, what do I care?' said Dan angrily, kicking over the bag of ash. 'It's only a parcel of dirt and a rusty old watch that don't go!'

He swung round furiously on his heel and walked away.

But next evening, when the Old Lord came to listen to the mice playing, he said,

'Why, bless my soul! That's the half-hunter watch that I lost when I was a boy. I'll have it cleaned up for you, old fellow, and then you won't have to worry about looking at the stable clock.'

When the watch was cleaned, it was as good as new. And the Old Lord hung it on its chain round Mr Mendelson's neck.

'There you are. Now, this watch is a *repeater* – if you press this knob, it will strike and tell you the time.

First it strikes the hour – ping. Then the quarters – ping, ping, ping. Then the minutes – ping, ping, ping, ping, ping. So, wherever you are, you will always know the time. You can press the knob with your chin.'

'Oh, hoy!' sighed Mr Mendelson. 'Sometimes I think this *time* is too much like hard work! Why did they have to invent it?'

But the mice were delighted with Mr Mendelson's watch. Bertha polished it every day and Gertrude wound it every night.

Dan Sligo was very angry indeed when he found he had let a perfectly good gold watch slip through his fingers. He went to Mr Mendelson and said,

'You're wearing my watch!'

'Oh, no, he isn't!' said Bertha, swinging on the watch-chain. 'It belongs to the Old Lord, and he has lent it to Mr Mendelson.'

'But if ever you want to know the time, we'll be pleased to tell you,' said Gertrude, and she pressed the knob of the watch, which instantly went ping-ping-ping-ping-ping, *ping*.

'Six o'clock. Music time,' said Bertha, leaping from Mr Mendelson's nose to the piano.

'Music time,' murmured Mr Mendelson, resting his chin on the keyboard. 'That's the best time of all!'

Mr Mendelson Goes
Backwards

It was a warm, wet, windy day in Spring. Cuckoos were seesawing in and out of the trees in Midnight Park.

For some reason old Mr Mendelson suddenly began hiccuping. Perhaps it was because he had eaten too much rich, green, indigestible grass. Or perhaps there were too many buttercups and daisies in the grass he had eaten. Or perhaps it was because he had been startled by a cuckoo, which had suddenly burst out of the oak tree just above his head and given a tremendously loud shout of 'Cuckoo!' right in his ear, just

as he was swallowing a large mouthful of mixed clover and campion. At any rate, for one of these reasons (or some other) Mr Mendelson, who was having his coat brushed by his two friends Bertha and Gertrude, all of a sudden let out such a violent hiccup – 'Hckcwkc-whoop!' – that both mice shot six inches into the air, and only saved themselves from falling down on to the grass by hanging tightly to Mr Mendelson's long black mane.

'Hckcwkcwhoop!' said Mr Mendelson again. But this time the mice were ready for it, and hung on to his coat with all their claws.

'I think you've got hiccups, Mr Mendelson,' said Gertrude politely.

'You've been eating too much green grass much too fast,' said Bertha, not so politely.

'Hckwckcwhoop!' said Mr Mendelson.

'Hiccups aren't caused by *grass*, excuse me, Bertha,' Gertrude contradicted her sister. 'Hiccups are caused when your heart gets out of time with your breath. Mr Mendelson's heart is going pit-a-pat, pit-a-pat, and he ought to breathe *in* on the pits, and *out* on the pats.' She laid her ear against his warm thick shaggy coat to listen to his heart. 'Instead of that –'

'Hckwckckwhoop!' said Mr Mendelson. Gertrude shot several feet into the air.

'*That's* not what causes hiccups,' said Bertha. 'Hiccups come from swallowing too suddenly, so that you get a bit of air caught in your swallow-tube –'

'Hckwckwhoop!' said Mr Mendelson.

'Never mind what *causes* the hiccups,' said Gertrude,

picking herself up from a mossy tree-stump where she had landed. 'The important thing is to cure them!'

She picked a large, wide blade of grass, and ran back, up Mr Mendelson's long tail and along his back, until she reached a spot just behind his ear. Then, holding the blade of grass sideways between her paws like a flute, she suddenly blew a very shrill earpiercing note on it – BLEEEE! – It sounded like a loud blast on a small trumpet made from potato-peel. Mr Mendelson nearly jumped out of his skin at the sudden unexpected loud noise right behind his ear.

'The way to cure somebody's hiccups is to give them a real fright,' Gertrude remarked complacently. 'You see, now he's better!'

'Hckwckwhoop!' said Mr Mendelson.

'*That* wasn't much use!' said Bertha to her sister. 'The *real* way to cure hiccups is to drink water and then throw your head back sharply. Come over to the pond, Mr Mendelson.'

Mr Mendelson obediently let the mice lead him over to the small pond. There he took a mouthful of water and threw his head back as he swallowed. But a hiccup came up and met the water as it went down; the water sprayed all over everything round about, including the mice.

'*That* wasn't much use,' said Gertrude, rubbing water out of her eyes. 'No, no, Bertha, the *best* way to cure hiccups is to drink water from the wrong side of the glass.'

'But, excuse me, Gertrude, we haven't *got* a glass.'

'So let him drink from the wrong side of the pond.'

'Which *is* the wrong side?' said Bertha.

'The other side from where he is, of course!'

So Mr Mendelson, standing on *this* side of the pond, reached across and took a swallow from the other side. (Luckily it was a very small pond – not much bigger than a bath-tub.) This time Mr Mendelson managed to keep the swallow down, but next minute he gave an extra-loud hiccup.

'HCKWCHCWHOOP?'

'This is becoming serious already,' said Gertrude. 'Maybe he ought to eat a dock-leaf standing on his head.'

'Maybe he should swallow a pail full of sugar while holding his breath.'

'Maybe he should touch his toes with his nose while saying the multiplication table.'

'Maybe he should sip vinegar from the wrong side of the spoon.'

'Ladies, ladies, please!' said Mr Mendelson. 'Isn't it bad enough – hckwckwchoop! – that I should have such an affliction which heaven knows – hckwchhck-whoop! – I never asked for – without your thinking of all these other ways to torture me?'

The mice took no notice of Mr Mendelson.

'Perhaps we should sting his nose with a nettle?'

'Get a squirrel to bite his ear?'

'Give him a spoonful of brandy with pepper in it?'

'Where are we going to get *brandy*?' objected Bertha.

'The Old Lord might have some.'

Bertha went off to find a nettle. Gertrude went to borrow some brandy from the Old Lord, who lived in an abandoned stable on the edge of the park.

At this moment the gipsy, Dan Sligo, came strolling into Midnight Park from the woods near by where he had his camp.

Ostensibly, Dan Sligo was pretending to fly a very large kite on the end of a very long rope, for he made kites and sold them, at high prices, to the local children. But in fact he was on the lookout for anything he could pick up, and especially for Mr Mendelson's piano, which stood under the oak tree, and on which the mice played beautiful tunes each evening at six o'clock.

Dan Sligo saw no reason why an old pony and two mice should have a piano all to themselves.

"Morning, Mr M,' said the gipsy, strolling up to Mr Mendelson, who was resting his chin on the piano.

'Hckwckwchoop!' said Mr Mendelson. All the strings inside the piano went twangle-twangle.

'Got hiccups, have-ee, then, Mr M?' said the gipsy sympathetically.

'Hckw . . .'

'Arr,' said Dan Sligo. 'I knows an easy cure for they hiccups. All you has to do is run as fast as 'ee can, *backwards*, in a straight line, as far as 'ee can go. That'll fix they pesky hickets – 'tis a sartain cure!'

By this time Mr Mendelson was getting very tired of the hiccups, and Dan Sligo's cure sounded more comfortable than the nettle or the brandy-and-pepper which Gertrude and Bertha were fetching. So he started walking backwards, rather slowly at first, because he had never gone backwards before, and he *was* over twenty, after all.

'Faster – 'ee must go a deal faster than that!' called the gipsy.

Mr Mendelson broke into a backwards trot.

'Canter – canter! Gallop, if 'ee can!' shouted Dan Sligo.

Mr Mendelson tried to canter, and splashed heavily into the pond. He was not going at all in a straight line.

'Faster – faster – that's the dandy! 'Ee be doing fine, real fine!' called Dan Sligo encouragingly. Then he tied the rope of his kite round Mr Mendelson's piano.

Just at that moment the mice returned, Gertrude dragging an enormous nettle, Bertha carefully carrying

a thimble full of brandy which she had borrowed from the Old Lord.

'Has Mr Mendelson gone crazy?' she demanded. 'Why is he running backwards?'

'Nay, 'tis a sartain cure for the hiccups,' Dan Sligo said, grinning.

'He'll hurt himself – he'll bump into a tree!' exclaimed Gertrude. 'Watch out, Mr Mendelson!'

Both mice laid down the things they were carrying and began to scamper after Mr Mendelson. But he was a long way off, by now, almost at the other end of the park, where the windmill stood. He was not keeping any kind of straight course, however; he would veer off very fast in one direction, then become anxious, rolling his eyes backwards in their sockets to try and see where he was going, and suddenly change his tack, so that he went along in a series of zigs and zags, hiccuping all the way.

'Wait, Mr Mendelson!' shouted the mice. 'Wait for us!'

At last, rushing as if the devil were after them, the mice caught up with Mr Mendelson, and ran up his legs. (It is not at all easy to climb up the legs of a pony who is running backwards, but they managed it, holding on grimly with their strong little claws.) Then, perched precariously on his rump, they were able to shout directions.

'More to the right, Mr Mendelson – haystack coming up on the left.'

'Straight – left a little – mind the cowpat!'

Mr Mendelson, who had great confidence in the mice, went much faster, and broke into a backwards gallop.

Meanwhile Dan Sligo had first drunk the thimble full of brandy, then taken two more turns of his rope round the piano, and let the kite out a little farther. The kite was high in the sky now, rollicking on a long slope of wind, way up among some white clouds. It lifted the piano two feet off the ground. Dan Sligo's plan was that the kite should carry the piano out of the park for him, while Mr Mendelson and the mice were kept distracted and a long way off by his cure for hiccups.

But just at this moment the Old Lord came rolling out of the stables in his wheelchair; he was curious to see if the brandy-and-pepper cure was working. He did not notice Mr Mendelson and the mice, who were nearly at the windmill by now – but he did see the piano, six feet up in the air at the end of the rope, and Dan Sligo guiding it along with his crooked stick.

'HEY!' shouted the Old Lord. 'You put that back!'

Dan Sligo, terribly startled, let go of the stick, and the kite twitched the piano up into the boughs of an oak tree, where it stuck. The rope snapped and the kite sailed off on the wind, who knows where.

Meanwhile the two mice, just as startled as Dan Sligo by the Old Lord's shout, had turned their heads to discover what was going on at the other end of the park. And the result of *that* was that Mr Mendelson, galloping backwards at full tilt, went straight through the open door of the windmill and ran slap into a pile of flour-sacks. One of them burst, letting out a suffocating cloud of white flour, which blew all over the mice and Mr Mendelson.

'Atchoo!'

'Bless you!'

'Katischoo!'

'Bless me!'

'Kertchoff!'

'Bless you!'

Sneezing, gasping and blinded, white with flour from tail to whiskers, the three of them finally managed to grope their way into the outside air, and shake some of the whiteness out of their eyes and noses.

When at last they got back to where Dan Sligo had been, they found the Old Lord, indignantly looking up at their piano, which was perched twenty feet out of reach among the branches of the oak tree.

'I shall have to send for Jim Thatcher and Robin Hedger to get it down with ladders,' he said.

'Oy, moy!' said Mr Mendelson. 'How did it get up *there*? Did the wind blow it up?'

'Wind?' said Bertha. 'More likely it was that thieving Dan Sligo! There he goes – over the park fence.'

'At any rate,' said Mr Mendelson, 'his cure has stopped my hiccups.'

Which was quite true!

Pastry in the Sky

Old Mr Mendelson spent a great deal of his time gazing at the sky. It was not very comfortable doing this, for his big head was balanced for looking down at the grass, or straight ahead; but just the same, he did it. When Gertrude or Bertha said, 'Watch out, Mr Mendelson! You'll trip over that dead branch! You're walking straight into the pond!' he would look down for a minute or two, but soon his head would go up again, and he would be staring at the clouds, which were shaped like fishbones – or like pancakes – or like leaves – or like loaves of bread – or like faraway hills.

'What *gives* them that shape?' he would murmur. 'What are they *doing* up there?'

'And I'll tell you another peculiar thing,' he said to Bertha and Gertrude. 'The sky has an amazing power. There's magic about it.'

'Rubbish!' said Bertha, briskly scrubbing out Mr Mendelson's ear with a bunch of dry grass. 'There's no such thing as magic.'

'Excuse *me*,' said Gertrude, polishing the gold watch that hung round Mr Mendelson's neck on a chain. This watch had a tiny glass window in front, about as big as your thumb-nail, through which you could see its face. And if you pressed the knob on top of the watch, it would tell you the time in a series of loud, sweet tings – first for the hour, then for the quarters after the hour,

then for the minutes after the quarter. Mr Mendelson could not see the watch where it hung on his chest, but he had learned to press the knob with his chin and so he could tell the time. The mice were very fond of the watch. They were always running up Mr Mendelson to have a look at it. And they kept it wound for him. Gertrude gave it a wind now, as she was talking.

'Excuse *me*, Bertha, but how do you know there isn't

any magic? There are plenty of things we don't understand. Maybe this watch is magic. What makes the hands go round? We don't know. What makes you think there's magic in the sky, Mr Mendelson?'

'You see that oak tree?' said Mr Mendelson. 'What colour is it?'

'Bright yellow,' said Bertha, looking up into the tree, which was gently dropping its leaves on them, for autumn had come to the big park where they lived.

'Right!' said Mr Mendelson triumphantly. 'And yet I can remember a time, long long ago, when it was dark green. And before that, it seems to me, it was pale green. And even longer ago, it seems to me, I can remember a time when there were no leaves on it at all.'

'So?' inquired Bertha, combing out his forelock with her tiny strong claws.

'So there's a magic in the sky which keeps changing the tree. Something we don't understand happens up there. And besides that, all kinds of things come *out* of the sky.'

'What things?' said Gertrude, brushing away at Mr Mendelson's coat with a bunch of thorn-twigs.

'Water. Bits of ice. Leaves,' said Mr Mendelson, as one fell on his nose. 'Birds. Branches. You never know what's going to come next.'

And he went on staring up at the stretches of blue, and the clouds moving across.

When the mice had finished tidying Mr Mendelson for the day, and had gone about their other affairs, the gipsy, Dan Sligo, came strolling over the grass, with a white pigeon sitting on his shoulder.

'Arternoon, Mr M!' said Dan Sligo. 'That surely is a handsome watch of yourn.'

'It belongs to the Old Lord really,' said Mr Mendelson. 'But he said that I could borrow it, as he has another.'

'I know that,' said Dan Sligo, who had found the

watch, lying in a wood, all covered with mould, and had given it to Mr Mendelson as a joke. But when the Old Lord had it cleaned and mended, Dan Sligo was very annoyed to find what a valuable object he had allowed to slip through his fingers. Now he had a plan to get it back again.

'Did you know,' said Dan Sligo idly, 'that if you

carry a thing high enough up into the sky, it will turn
into pastry?'

For Dan had overheard a bit of Mr Mendelson's
conversation with the mice.

'What sort of things?' said Mr Mendelson.

He didn't entirely trust Dan Sligo, but he couldn't
help being interested.

'What sort of things? Well – your watch, for instance.
If that watch was carried high into the sky, it would
turn into pastry.'

Mr Mendelson was sorry Bertha and Gertrude were
not there. He felt sure that Bertha would say, 'Rubbish!' But he himself was not quite certain about it.

'How *could* you take my watch up into the sky?' he
said doubtfully.

'Why,' said Dan Sligo, stroking his white pigeon.
'My old Cooey could do it in a minute, couldn't you,
Cooey?'

'Vrrrc, rrrrkty coo,' said Cooey.

'I'll show you, shall I?' said Dan Sligo. 'We'll just
take your watch off –' and he did so, unfastening the
gold chain, 'I'll put the chain in my pocket, that'd
make it too heavy for Cooey –' and he did this too, very
quickly, so that Mr Mendelson could hardly see his
hands move, 'now Cooey takes the watch in her beak –
I toss her up high, to give her a start – and you'll see!'

With a big swing of his arm Dan Sligo tossed Cooey
into the air, while old Mr Mendelson was still trying to
think of a polite way to say, 'No thank you, I'd rather
you didn't.'

Up and up, round and round, went Cooey, fluttering

and flickering like a white paper bag against the blue of the autumn sky.

Mr Mendelson watched with great anxiety. His neck felt very bare without the gold chain and the round gold watch hanging from it.

'Cooey won't *drop* the watch, will she?' he said.

'Lord bless ye, no!' Dan Sligo said cheerfully,

slapping his pocket. 'That watch'll come to no harm. Ol' Cooey's as safe as the Newcastle mail-coach. Don't ye fret about Cooey. She'll bring the watch back sure enough – but it'll be made o' pastry.'

Up and up went Cooey, until she seemed to be almost touching the sun, she was so high and far up above the top of the golden oak tree.

Then she began slowly circling down again. Round and round she went, round and round and round, as if she were on a blue stream of water running out of a giant bath plug-hole.

At last she came to rest on Dan Sligo's shoulder. And – sure enough – she was holding in her beak a round flat watch made of hard shiny pastry, glazed brown with egg-white.

Mr Mendelson was very amazed. Dan Sligo – who had made the pastry himself – was not so surprised.

'There!' he said triumphantly. 'What did I tell ye? Try a bit, Mr Mendelson! Ye'll find it rale good pastry – the best ye ever laid lip to!'

And he held out the pastry watch temptingly on the palm of his hand. For, he thought, once it had been eaten up, Mr Mendelson could hardly ask for his watch back.

Mr Mendelson, however, looked at the pastry watch very doubtfully. Then he smelt it carefully.

'Oy!' he said. 'Who'd have believed it! May a forest grow on my back! What next? It seems the sky does turn things into pastry. Wasn't I just saying to Bertha and Gertrude that it had remarkable power? But – excuse me – I would rather have my watch back the

way it was before. What use to me is a pastry watch, if you please?'

'Oh I'm afraid *that's* not possible,' said Dan Sligo cheerfully. 'Once pastry, always pastry! D'you think you can turn pastry back into flour and water? Or flour back into corn? Or corn into seed? You think you can turn an oak tree into an acorn? You think you can turn Cooey back into an egg?'

'Vrrrrc, rkkkty coo,' said Cooey.

'Excuse *me*,' said old Mr Mendelson very politely. 'I don't know about such things. And in any case, who *wants* to turn Cooey into an egg? All I want is my gold watch back, for it belongs to the Old Lord.'

'I'm sorry,' said Dan Sligo – he didn't sound it, however – 'but ye should ha' thought o' that afore ye asked me to let ol' Cooey take it up into the sky. Now it's turned to pastry there's naught for it but to eat it.

Eating's just about all a pastry watch is good for. But ye'll find it a rale tempting tidbit, Mr Mendelson.'

Mr Mendelson was quite put out.

'Who needs a pastry watch? I want it about as much as I want shoes made out of sugar.'

'Can't help that,' said Dan Sligo. 'You've got it now.' And he still held out the watch on the palm of his hand.

When Mr Mendelson had a problem he always called for his friends Bertha and Gertrude. So now he lifted up his head and whinnied.

'Oyyyy, Bertha! Oyyyy! Gertrude! Would you be so kind as to come here a moment, please, ladies, if you are not otherwise occupied? There's a pastry watch here I'd like your opinion about.'

Gertrude and Bertha, who had been laying out their bedding (which was made from Mr Mendelson's thick furry undercoat) in the sun to air, stopped work and came scampering across the grass.

'Oh-oh,' muttered Dan Sligo. 'Here comes trouble! Why do these pesky little nibblers have to come along poking their needle-noses into other people's business? Who needs *them*?'

'What's the matter, Mr Mendelson?' asked the mice, running up Mr Mendelson's tail and along his back on to his forehead.

'You see Dan Sligo here?' said the pony. 'He has changed my watch into pastry.'

'How did he do that?' said Gertrude.

'By having Cooey fly up into the sky with it. And now he says he can't change it back.'

'That sounds like rubbish to me,' said Bertha.

'Is it *good* pastry?' said Gertrude, and she ran down Mr Mendelson's nose towards Dan Sligo's hand, which once more held out the pastry watch invitingly.

But just at that moment the real watch, which Dan Sligo had hidden in his waistcoat pocket, let out three silvery notes – ting, ting, ting! Three o'clock! For as Dan bent forward, the knob of the watch had pressed against a silver snuffbox, which he also kept in his pocket.

Both mice knew *that* sound as well as they knew their own voices.

'Humph!' muttered Bertha. 'We certainly do seem to have a few mysteries around here! For a start, we've got a watch that can throw its voice.'

Quick as butter in a hot pan she ran down Mr Mendelson's nose, skipped across on to Dan Sligo's cuff, ran up his shirtsleeve, and dived head first into his waistcoat pocket.

In a moment she reappeared, dragging Mr Mendelson's gold watch by its handle.

'Oy, oy, just look what I found!' she shouted triumphantly, panting with her efforts. Then she added with great politeness, 'I think you perhaps made a little mistake, Mr Sligo? Gertrude, just step over here a moment, could you, and pull out the chain? That's in here as well. Maybe Mr Sligo forgot he had them in his pocket.'

Gertrude sprang from Mr Mendelson's nose to Dan's waistcoat button, and pulled out the long gold chain.

'That's odd,' murmured Mr Mendelson. 'That's very

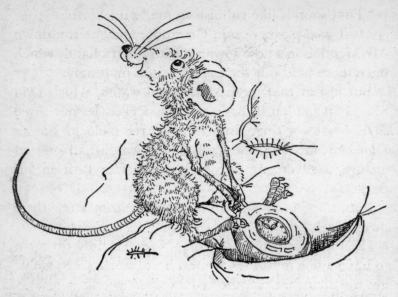

singular. How did my watch and chain get into Dan Sligo's waistcoat pocket?'

Red-faced, very much annoyed, Dan Sligo dumped the two mice, with the watch and chain, down on the grass. He dropped the pastry watch at the same time.

'Mice!' he muttered. 'Why the plague, I ask you, doesn't some cat gobble them up? I never could abide the nasty little creatures.'

And he turned and stamped off across the grass, grumbling to himself all the way, while the mice fastened the watch and chain round Mr Mendelson's neck once more.

Then they ate up the pastry watch, since Dan Sligo did not seem to want it.

'Very good,' they said, nibbling quickly round the edges. 'Won't you try a bit, Mr Mendelson?'

But Mr Mendelson was not to be tempted.

'Eat and enjoy it my dear friends. But don't ask *me* to touch anything that comes out of the sky. Didn't I tell you there was something very peculiar going on up there?'

Managing Without the Moon

Besides beautiful music, Mr Mendelson was particularly fond of the moon. He loved to watch it when, sometimes, in daytime, it floated across the sky like a white balloon, looking puzzled and lost, as if it were not sure of the way home. And, even better, Mr Mendelson loved the moon at night, when it shone bright as silver and made all the trees in the park throw long shadows across the grass.

Every day, when Mr Mendelson's two friends the fieldmice Bertha and Gertrude were brushing and combing him all over, pulling the prickles and burrs out of his thick shaggy coat, plaiting his mane, teasing and stroking out his long tail with their tiny clever claws, they held long argumentative conversations.

The mice were much better informed than Mr Mendelson, because they sometimes went out of the park and under the town, in their tunnels, and they talked to the town mice and heard all the news.

Whereas Mr Mendelson never went anywhere, now that he was so old; sometimes he just stood in one spot for hours together. But he thought a lot, all the time he was standing still.

'So what is the moon?' he asked Bertha one day, when she was brushing out his forelock.

The moon was floating overhead at the time, like a large white soap-bubble.

'The moon?' said Bertha, holding a tuft of forelock

between her strong little claws, while she pulled out a
thorn with her teeth, and spat it away. 'Pffft! Excuse
me! The moon's a silver shilling.'

'Excuse *me*!' said Gertrude, who was brushing Mr
Mendelson's ears, 'but the moon is *not* a silver shilling.
It is a cream cracker. That's why it gets smaller all the
time. Somebody is eating it up there. You could not eat
a silver shilling.'

'Pardon *me*: it is a shilling.'

'*No*, Bertha. It is a plain biscuit.'

'Whichever it is,' said Mr Mendelson, 'why doesn't
it fall down?'

'Because the sky is sticky. Like honey.'

'Sticky like jam,' said Gertrude. Both mice were

agreed about that. 'The sky is so sticky that all kinds of things get stuck up there. Like sheep's wool on bramble bushes. In fact there *is* quite a lot of sheep's wool in the sky.'

'That's true,' said Mr Mendelson looking at the clouds floating past.

'There you are, Mr Mendelson! Now you're done for the day,' said Bertha, sliding down his tail, while Gertrude gave a last polish to his shoes. 'Go and look at yourself in the pond.'

There was a tiny round pond in the park where Mr Mendelson lived with the mice. It was not much larger than a round table, and the grass came right to its edge.

Mr Mendelson walked slowly over to the pond and looked into it. There were some red and brown leaves floating about on the water, for autumn had come. Mr Mendelson could see his own reflection looking up at him. His coat was all black and shiny, because the mice had given him such a good brushing.

And then, suddenly, he saw something else in the pond.

'Bertha – Gertrude!' he called anxiously. 'Come here – quick! A bad thing has happened! The moon has fallen into the pond!'

Both mice came scampering to the water's edge and looked in. But now a whole patch of dead leaves had floated across the pond. There was nothing to be seen. The moon's reflection had gone.

'Oh, the moon has sunk down to the bottom, right into the mud!' mourned Mr Mendelson. 'We shall never see it again.'

He looked up at the sky, where clouds were beginning to gather. Sure enough, no moon was there.

'It will float up again,' prophesied Gertrude. 'Biscuits do float, after all.'

'*No*, excuse *me*, Gertrude. It is a shilling, and shillings do *not* float.'

That night it was very cold. Even inside his warm, thick coat, Mr Mendelson felt the cold in his old bones, and shivered in his sleep. Although the cold did not wake him, it made him dream. He dreamed about the gipsy, Dan Sligo, who lived in the woods on the edge of the park, and caught rabbits and cut clothes pegs and stole vegetables from people's gardens. Dan Sligo had a very clever lurcher dog called Jess, who was trained to pick up anything she found and take it back to her master. Jess had been taught to catch fish, too, and could snap a trout from the stream in her jaws without breaking a single one of its scales.

In the old pony's dream he saw Dan Sligo by the pond with a fishing-net; he saw the dog Jess dash into the water and come out with the moon in her teeth and give it to her master. Then the gipsy dropped the moon into his net and slung it over his shoulder and walked away.

'Oy, moy, Dan Sligo has stolen the moon!' mourned Mr Mendelson in his sleep, and woke himself up. He was so cold, and so worried by his dream, that although it was hardly morning yet, he made his way to the pond, which was some distance from where he had been sleeping with his chin resting on the keyboard of his beloved piano. The weather was bitterly cold. As Mr Mendelson moved along, his hoofs went scrunch, scrunch, through the grass, which was white with frost.

When Mr Mendelson came close to the pond, what did he see? He saw Dan Sligo, with an axe, very busy, hacking away, all round the rim of the pond. The strokes of the axe made a loud splintering sound in the silent frosty park, which was all grey with early-morning light.

Dan Sligo saw the old pony coming slowly across the white crisp grass.

'How do, Mr Mendelson!' he called cheerfully. 'Up early, ain't 'ee? Don't sleep so good these sharp nights, eh? Ancient bones gets to creaking in the frost, divvn't they? Best ask the Old Lord for a blanket.'

'What are you doing, Dan Sligo?' asked Mr Mendelson. He was very worried at seeing the gipsy working by the pond where the moon lay drowned. His heart went geflip, geflap.

'What am I a-doing?' The gipsy winked. 'Best ask Mr Brown the pastrycook how he makes his ice-cream! A frozen tongue can't tell 'ee no lie, Mr Mendelson!'

And at that, Dan Sligo did an amazing thing. He gave a tilting push to the surface of the pond with his foot. He gave a pull with his arms. And the whole pond seemed to tip sideways in a great white circle. Dan Sligo tipped up the white circle on to its edge, and began to roll it away over the grass.

Mr Mendelson watched him go with starting eyes. 'Stop! Stop! Come back, Dan Sligo!' he called faintly. But the gipsy took no notice. He rolled his round of white over the grass to the park fence where he had a hand-barrow waiting, tipped forward on its wheel. He rolled the white circle straight into the barrow. And

then he pushed the barrow away down the hill into the town.

When the two mice arrived, later in the morning, to brush Mr Mendelson's coat, they found the old pony very sad and silent.

'What's the matter, Mr Mendelson?' said Bertha, running up on to his nose, for his head hung down so low that it was an easy jump from a frosty clump of grass. 'Why are you so gloomy?'

'Dan Sligo was here early this morning, and he has

stolen the moon out of our pond, and rolled it away down the hill.'

'You're pulling my tail!' gasped Gertrude. 'Stolen the moon? Dan Sligo? Oy, what a scoundrel! Why has he done that?'

'Why ask why? That sneak would steal the egg from his mother's breakfast if he thought he could get it away without her noticing,' said Bertha. 'Of course he'll sell it to somebody. But who would buy the moon?'

'He said something about Mr Brown the pastrycook,' said Mr Mendelson sadly. 'He said, "Ask Mr Brown how he makes his ice-cream." What do you think he meant by that? What *is* ice-cream?'

Even the well-informed mice didn't know that. But they promised Mr Mendelson that they would find out, when they had finished tidying him for the day; they would go and visit their cousins Martha and Charlotte, who lived under Mr Brown's shop and made use of his cake-crumbs.

All day Mr Mendelson wandered sorrowfully about the park. It was a grey cloudy day, very cold. He hardly did more than nibble at the frosty grass. Many, many times he peered sadly into the pond. Often, often, he gazed up at the sky. But no moon was to be seen in either place.

At six o'clock the mice returned and climbed up Mr Mendelson's tail on to the piano, for it was time to play their evening concert. But first, Mr Mendelson was anxious to know what they had found out from their cousins.

'Well? Well? How *does* Mr Brown the pastrycook make his ice-cream?'

'He has a big wooden machine, as big as a barrel, and he turns a handle round and round and round. And he opens the top and scoops out the ice-cream.'

'Yes? So what is this ice-cream?'

'Charlotte and Martha stole a crumb for us to try. It is round and cold and white, and it melts on your whiskers before you have a chance to taste it,' said Bertha.

'I'm afraid it's quite clear that ice-cream is made from melted moon,' sighed Gertrude.

'Oy, moy!' lamented Mr Mendelson. 'We shall never see our beautiful moon again. Dan Sligo has stolen it and Mr Brown has ground it up and made it into ice-cream.'

The two mice looked at each other and shook their heads.

'For once, Mr Mendelson,' said Bertha, 'I'm afraid you are right.'

They all sat grieving for the moon in silence. Then Gertrude said, 'Well, tears won't fry pancakes. Let's play a bit of music and try to cheer up. Just because the moon is gone, is that a reason to mope?'

'No – you are right,' said her sister. 'We'll have to learn to manage without the moon.'

And without waiting any longer the two mice began scampering up and down the keyboard of the piano, pressing down the black notes and the white, using their noses, their feet, and even their tails, with terrific dexterity and energy. They made such brilliant

and glorious music that the Old Lord, who lived in the
stables, heard it, and came rolling himself across the
park in his wheelchair to listen and enjoy it at closer
quarters.

'Now play the moonlight piece,' said Mr Mendelson,
when it was nearly time to stop.

The moonlight piece was his favourite, his particular
favourite, for it was slow and thoughtful, moving along
at a quiet dreamy pace like the moon gently drifting
through the branches of trees, throwing one shadow
after another.

As Mr Mendelson listened to it, a tear rolled down
each side of his nose. He thought to himself, 'I shall
never see the moon again. The nights will always be
dark from now on.'

But then – all of a sudden – he noticed that the tears
rolling down his nose each had a silvery dot of moon
reflected in them. And when he raised his head, there

was the moon itself, just climbing out of a hawthorn bush.

'Bertha! Getrude!' he shouted. 'Look! Look! The moon has come back! Your music must have put it together again!'

All three of them sat gazing in silent amazement as the moon disentangled itself from the bush and moved up into the sky.

Then the Old Lord said, 'Well, well, it's my bedtime. And it's your bedtime too, Mr Mendelson. I brought your blanket tonight. Winter's just around the corner.' And he buckled a warm tartan blanket around the old pony's barrel-stomach, before rolling himself away in his wheelchair.

'What did he mean, winter is just around the corner?' said Gertrude.

'Maybe he meant, just around the cornfield,' suggested Bertha.

'Well anyway,' said Mr Mendelson, 'now we know for certain what the moon is made of. The moon is made of ice-cream. And at least we know, too, that if Dan Sligo should steal it again, you can always get it back with your music.'

So that night Mr Mendelson slept soundly in his blanket, without a single dream. And the mice slept soundly in their mouse-hole, which was warmly lined with combings from Mr Mendelson's thick coat.

Overhead, the moon drifted through the sky, and what it was made of, who can say?

The Fiery Christmas Trees

One autumn day there was a lot of unusual activity in Midnight Park. At the north end of the park, which was farthest from the town, dozens of men were digging hundreds of holes. The Old Lord went to watch them, rolling himself over the grass in his wheelchair.

Mr Mendelson was being given his daily brush-down by Bertha and Gertrude.

'Look at those great wagons coming into the park,' said Gertrude, disentangling a knot in Mr Mendelson's mane.

'Look at the size of the horses pulling them!' said Bertha. 'They make Mr Mendelson look like a foal.'

Mr Mendelson walked up to the north end of the park to see what was happening, while his two friends busily went on with their work.

Out of the wagons, which were drawn by huge shirehorses, the men were unloading many, many little fir-trees, and these were carefully planted in the holes which had already been dug for them.

At last every tree was in place, the tools were loaded back into the wagons, the drivers cracked their whips, and the great horses broke into a slow trot. Soon everybody was gone, except for Mr Mendelson, thoughtfully blowing air down his long nose, and the two mice, and the Old Lord, who sat in his wheelchair looking round him at all the little trees.

'Well, Mr Mendelson,' said the Old Lord. 'One day

this will be a forest of trees as tall as the stable clock-tower. I shan't be here to see it,' he said, sighing, 'and you won't see it, Mr Mendelson, for trees take a long time to grow – but young Sam will see it.'

Young Sam was the Old Lord's grandson, who was away at school.

'Young Sam will be home before that, though,' the Old Lord went on kindly, noticing that Mr Mendelson looked rather sad at the mention of his name. 'Yes, he'll be home in a couple of months to give you your Christmas apple. And he'll have a Christmas tree too. But not one of these. No, no – these trees will be allowed to grow tall; perhaps they will be the masts of ships in fifty years' time, Mr Mendelson.'

And the Old Lord, having satisfied himself that all his little trees were safely settled, rolled away in his wheelchair, back to the stables.

'What are Christmas trees?' Mr Mendelson asked the mice, who had finished his coat by now and were brushing his furry ears.

'We've told you about Christmas trees dozens of times,' said Bertha severely.

'So tell me again! Oy, my! I find it hard to remember things, now I'm so old,' sighed Mr Mendelson. Really he just liked hearing about Christmas trees.

'Young Sam has a Chrstmas tree every year. So do all the children in the town. The trees are covered with gold and silver, and with red and blue and green fruits.'

'And nuts,' put in Gertrude.

'And nuts, of course, and raisins and oranges and coloured flowers.'

'That I should like to see,' said Mr Mendelson. 'Why don't they do it to all the trees in the park?'

'It only happens to trees *inside* houses,' said Gertrude.

'That's not true, excuse me,' said Bertha. 'Sometimes the big tree in the town square is all covered with shining things at Christmas.'

'Well, anyway, it never happens to trees in this park,' said Gertrude.

A week or so after the trees were planted, a surprising thing did happen in the park, however. The two mice were playing their evening music to Mr Mendelson on his piano when, over at the south end, near the town, a whole fountain of wonderful sparkling lights suddenly shot up into the black night sky.

'Oy! May the wind blow me away!' exclaimed Mr Mendelson. 'Bertha! Gertrude! Look at the sky! Did you ever see such a sight?'

For once, the mice stopped playing their beautiful tunes on Mr Mendelson's piano and watched with their mouths wide open as more and more lines and

circles and clusters and cascades of lights climbed up into the sky. Some of the lights were like flowers, and some were like birds or ships flying through the air. Gertrude and Bertha leapt from the piano on to Mr Mendelson's back, and he trotted down to the south end of the park so that they could watch what was happening from near at hand.

'Tchkk! Tchkk!' said Bertha. 'One thing you can be sure of – there's always something going on in this park.'

Near the south end of the park they found the Old Lord in his wheelchair.

'Come to watch the fireworks, Mr Mendelson?' he said. 'I wouldn't go too close or a spark might singe your coat!'

So Mr Mendelson stood still and watched a beautiful waterfall of yellow and silver sparks, which poured up into the air and then peeled back in curving lines, as if somebody were drawing pine-trees on the sky with a gold pencil.

'I know what those are,' he said to the mice. 'Those are Christmas trees.'

'No, no *no*!' said Bertha testily. '*Those* aren't Christmas trees.'

'Christmas trees are *completely* different,' said Gertrude.

'But you said that Christmas trees were covered with gold and silver. And they are just the shape of trees.'

'Well they aren't Christmas trees!'

'It's no use trying to explain to him,' said Bertha. 'You'll see a real Christmas tree some time, Mr Mendelson, and then you'll understand.'

'Don't do me any favours!' said the old pony. 'I'd rather have these beautiful gold trees up in the sky.'

He stood gazing and gazing upwards, while the mice, who always wanted to know how things were done, looked sharply about and noticed how children tied their fireworks to sticks and lit them, how they went up, and how the burnt-out cases and sticks fell back and thumped on the ground after the fireworks had burst in lights and colours up in the air.

At last the show was over and everybody went home to bed.

68

Now winter had come to the park. The birds were silent all day long, sitting huddled up in their feathers.

Sometimes snow fell. But Mr Mendelson stayed warm in his thick blanket, which the Old Lord had strapped round his middle, and the two mice kept warm by scampering about, or by energetically playing Mr Mendelson's piano. At night they were snug in their nest, which was lined with fur from Mr Mendelson's thick shaggy coat. And although there was not much food in the park, sometimes the Old Lord rolled over in his wheelchair with a bundle of hay, or a handful of oats, which Mr Mendelson shared with the mice.

Then, late one cold night, long after the mice had played their night music on Mr Mendelson's piano and gone to nest, they were suddenly woken again by Mr Mendelson blowing down their mouse-hole.

'Oy, Bertha! Oy, Gertrude! Something bad is happening in the park!'

'Mr Mendelson! Why are you waking us in the middle of the night? What's the matter? Have you got a pain? Did your blanket fall off? Did you have a nightmare? Why are you blowing down our hole? It's not morning yet!'

The two mice came scrambling out of their hole, rather crossly, for the air outside was very cold indeed.

'Listen!' said Mr Mendelson. He was very excited and upset. 'Listen – Dan Sligo the gipsy has come into the park with some other men and a big cart drawn by two horses. I heard the horses whinny, so I went up to the north end of the park to see what they were doing.'

'And what *are* they doing?' yawned Gertrude.

But Bertha looked very wide-awake at once, for Dan Sligo was a notorious thief, who could steal somebody's bed while they were asleep, and leave them with nothing but the pillow-case.

'They are stealing all the Old Lord's little trees! They are digging them up and putting them in the cart. And I heard Dan Sligo say that he was going to sell them for Christmas trees.'

'But that's very bad!' said Bertha. 'The Old Lord wants them to grow into a forest. Those men ought to get their Christmas trees somewhere else.'

'But how are we going to stop them taking these ones?' said Mr Mendelson.

'We could wake the Old Lord. If he weren't so deaf.'

'But he *is* so deaf,' said Mr Mendelson. 'Already I

neighed and whinnied and stamped outside his window and he didn't wake.'

'If only he *would* wake,' said Gertrude thoughtfully, 'he could shoot his blunderbuss at those men and frighten them away. How can we make a loud enough noise to scare those men?'

'I know!' said Bertha. 'The fireworks. The fireworks made a lot of noise!'

'How do you mean the fireworks, idiot?' said her sister, giving her a bite. 'The fireworks were *weeks* ago.'

'Yes, but there are some left, don't you remember? We found some that never got used, hidden in a hollow tree.'

'But you have to set light to them. How are you going to do that?'

This was a hard question. Both mice frowned and knitted their whiskers for some time, while Mr Mendelson stood chewing a hank of grass.

'We need fire,' said Gertrude.

'We haven't got any,' said Bertha.

Mr Mendelson chewed a bit more. Then he said, 'The hedge-cutters were burning all the hedge-clippings in a big bonfire this afternoon.'

'So they were!' said Gertrude, giving his ear a loving tweak. 'Good for you, Mr Mendelson. Let's go and see if there's any fire left.'

So Mr Mendelson carried the two mice to the big black patch near the hedge, where all afternoon a fire of brushwood and brambles and twigs had fiercely burned.

With great care the two mice poked and raked among the blackened ashes. At last Bertha shouted, 'I've found a bit. I've found a twig which shines red when I blow on it!'

'Bring it here quickly, then,' said Mr Mendelson.

So the two mice scurried up his tail, Bertha carrying the glowing twig, and Gertrude blowing on it to keep it bright.

'Mind you don't singe Mr Mendelson's tail!'

'Can't you see that I'm carrying it as far away as I can?'

Mr Mendelson trotted as fast as he could to the hollow tree where, by mistake, some children had left a whole bag of unused fireworks.

Bertha carefully slid the glowing twig underneath the paper bag.

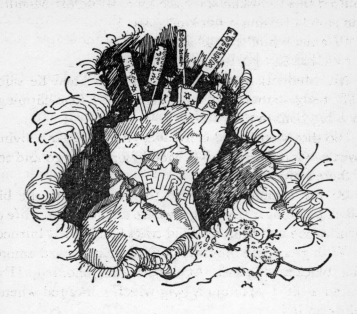

'Now we'd better go away quickly,' she said. 'We don't want any of those fireworks to bump into *us*. Besides, we want to see if the noise frightens Dan Sligo.'

'Suppose the fireworks don't light up?' said Mr Mendelson.

'Let's worry about one thing at a time!'

So the mice ran back up Mr Mendelson's tail and he carried them towards where the new little trees had been planted.

Just as they were passing the stable, *Whizz! Whoosh! Whumpf! Cracketa-cracket! Smack! Geshwoff!* All the fireworks burst out of the tree together, and the tree, which was only an old hollow stump, went with them into the

73

air. The sky was full of golden rain and about a hundred tremendously loud bangs exploded at the same moment. There was so much noise, indeed, that even the Old Lord woke up, and came rolling out of the stable in his wheelchair to see what was going on.

He found Mr Mendelson just outside, looking at the sky in amazement, and the two mice on his back, huddling together with their paws over their ears.

'What are you *doing*, what in the name of goodness is *happening*?' said the Old Lord indignantly. 'Do you *have* to fight the battle of Waterloo just outside my window?'

The sky was still full of exploding fireworks, and by their light, which coloured the whole park bright yellow, the Old Lord saw the wagon and horses, and Dan Sligo, and the men with spades and hatchets, interrupted in their work of stealing the little Christmas trees.

'HEY! YOU!' shouted the Old Lord, in a voice like thunder. 'You stop that – before I get out my blunderbuss and blow you all into bramble jelly!'

The thieves were so terrified that they jumped into their wagon and drove off at a gallop, leaving their tools behind – not to mention the trees they had dug up.

Next day the Old Lord had all his trees carefully replanted in the holes from which they had been taken. All except for one. And that he had planted by Mr Mendelson's piano.

'There! That one's for you, Mr Mendelson,' said the Old Lord. 'And for Bertha and Gertrude. That's for saving my forest.'

Next month, when Christmas Day came, and young Sam was home from school, the little fir-tree by the piano was decorated all over with gold and silver tinsel, and sugared apples and nuts and oranges and raisins. So that year Gertrude, Bertha and Mr Mendelson had a Christmas tree of their very own.

Looking After Rosa

Just before he went back to school for the autumn term, little Sam came to say good-bye to Mr Mendelson. It was a fine, sunny September day; the starlings were chittering and gargling in the oak tree under which Mr Mendelson kept his piano, and Bertha and Gertrude were hard at work collecting little piles of acorns and beech-nuts.

'I've come to ask a favour, Mr Mendelson,' said little Sam, giving the old pony a hug. 'While I'm away, would you very kindly keep an eye on Rosa for me? Otherwise she might feel a bit lonely. Grandfather says he's too old to look after a bird.'

Rosa was a tumbler pigeon. She had been given to little Sam for his birthday six weeks ago, by Tim Lee, the blacksmith in the village, who bred pigeons in his spare time. Rosa was white, with pink eyes like spindle-berries; she had a very fat chest and a very silly giggling coo. She giggled most of the time. Tim Lee swore that she could fly a hundred miles an hour, but nobody had ever seen her go at even a quarter of that speed.

'Pigeons are not allowed at my school,' little Sam explained to Mr Mendelson. 'You won't have to worry about feeding her, because she can fly into the stable-loft through the hole where there's a tile missing in the roof, and I've left a sack of grain there for her. So all you have to do is talk to her and keep an eye on her.'

Mr Mendelson was not very happy at being asked to keep an eye on Rosa.

Look after a pigeon?

How was he supposed to do that?

But while he was collecting his slow old wits to say: 'Excuse me: I don't think I *know* how to look after a pigeon,' little Sam gave him another hug and ran off to the wagonette which was waiting to take him to the station.

Mr Mendelson stood thoughtfully staring after the wagonette as it rolled away, and Rosa sat on top of his head, cooing softly to herself. She was still there ten minutes later when Bertha and Gertrude arrived to give him his daily brush-down.

'Why is Rosa sitting on your head, Mr Mendelson?' inquired Bertha briskly, combing the old pony's mane with a teazel.

'Little Sam asked me to keep an eye on her,' Mr Mendelson said doubtfully.

He could feel Rosa's prickly toenails digging into his scalp, and he was rather dismayed at the thought of

having them there for the next three months, until Sam came home for Christmas.

However just at that moment Rosa launched herself into the air, and flew up to the topmost twig of the oak tree, where she perched, bending down the twig into a hoop with her substantial weight.

'Oy – *Rosa*!' shouted Mr Mendelson, very agitated. 'Don't go so *high*! You might fall!'

'Vrrrrreroo!' giggled Rosa gaily in reply. 'Ricketty coo!'

She sat swaying about on the thin twig, puffing out her white chest in the sunshine. And she showed no sign whatever of any intention to obey Mr Mendelson.

'Am I glad that *I* don't have to look after that nitwit!' muttered Bertha, brushing away at Mr Mendelson's mane. 'I don't believe she's got so much as two ideas in her noddle. All she can do is coo.'

'Oh well, I daresay she can take care of herself,' said Gertrude, watching Rosa, who was now performing some complicated antics in the air up above them, pretending to fall, and then fluttering up at the last moment, just before she seemed bound to hit the ground. 'She certainly knows some fancy ways of flying.'

'Rosa! Take care!' shouted Mr Mendelson in alarm. 'You had better come back and sit on my head.'

'Coo to you!' giggled Rosa, fluttering up into the oak tree once more.

'Take no notice, she's just showing off,' sniffed Bertha. 'You shouldn't worry your head about that one, Mr Mendelson.'

But Mr Mendelson did worry his head about Rosa all day long. All through the day he followed her nervously about the park, keeping an eye on her as she flew.

'Rosa – you are driving me out of my mind! Will you please not go so high? Will you please sit where I can keep an eye on you?'

'Rosa! That branch is definitely not strong enough to bear your weight!'

'Rosa! Watch out! There's a big bird in the chestnut tree – I think it might be a hawk. Please come down here directly!'

'Oh, *Rosa*! You are flying too fast – where do you think you are off to? At that speed you will be outside the park in a minute!'

Not a bit of attention did Rosa pay, to any of Mr Mendelson's anxious cries. She cooed her giggling coo, and went her own way regardless. By teatime the old pony was quite exhausted with anxiety and trotting about after the wayward pigeon.

At six, Mr Mendelson tried to put Rosa out of his mind. He pulled the rope which was passed over a branch of the oak tree and attached to the waterproof cover of his piano. This raised up the cover, and then Mr Mendelson opened the keyboard lid with his chin. And then the two fieldmice gave a concert, playing wonderful tunes on the piano – fast tunes, slow tunes, joyful dancing tunes, sad haunting tunes – sometimes both mice played together, sometimes one played on her own while the other took a rest. Usually Mr Mendelson listened to their music in rapture, with his chin resting on the end of the keyboard; but today he was too worried about Rosa, who had flown to the top of the oak tree above their heads.

However, halfway through the concert she came flopping down through the branches – flap – crash – flump – scuffle – wallop – and perched on a branch directly above the piano. Then she shut her eyes – taking no notice of the music – and went to sleep.

'Let's hope that's all the trouble you'll be having from her for the day,' grumbled Bertha (watching her sister perform a terrific leap, in order to follow one note very quickly by another which was about twenty inches away on the keyboard – ping! – *pong*!) 'Poor Mr Mendelson's quite worn out with the worry. What a thing! – to saddle him with such a responsibility.'

Indeed the poor old pony was so tired that his eyes were closing and his head was nodding by the end of the concert; he stayed awake long enough to pull the cover back over the piano, and then he went straight off to sleep where he stood.

When he woke up next morning the first thing he did was to look for Rosa. And his first sight of her made him give a loud gulp of horror.

'Oy, my stars! *Bertha! Gertrude!* Come here quickly! Rosa has died in the night! She's dead! Oh my, oh my, whatever shall I say to little Sam?'

'What? What's that? What's the matter, Mr Mendelson?'

Shaking their whiskers and rubbing their eyes, the two mice came scrambling out of their hole.

'*Now* what's up?' grumbled Gertrude, who was not at her best in the morning.

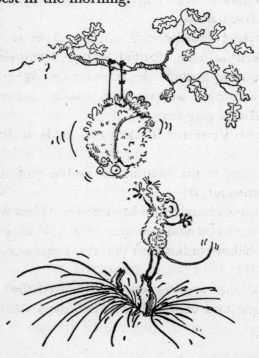

Then they stared, following the direction of Mr Mendelson's horrified eyes.

Rosa was hanging upside down from an oak twig, perfectly motionless, like a stuffed bird.

'May I be munched up by an owl!' gasped Bertha. 'Rosa! *Rosa!* Wake up! What's *with* you, hanging upside down like a hank of birdseed?'

'Go and stand underneath her, Mr Mendelson!' directed Gertrude, practically.

Mr Mendelson walked over and looked up in horror at the dangling pigeon. But Gertrude, tip-toe on the top of one of Mr Mendelson's ears, just below the upside-down Rosa, screamed as loud as she could, in a shrill voice like a factory siren,

'WAKE UP, ROSA!'

To everybody's relief, this worked. Rosa shook herself, croaked a little, fluffed out her feathers, and suddenly swung round like a gymnast. Whizz! And there she was, right way up on her twig, looking down at them all and giggling.

'Vrrrrrro! Vrrrrrro! Ricketty coo! Is it breakfast time?'

Off she flew to the hole in the stable roof, and disappeared through it.

'Well I never!' said Mr Mendelson. 'Bless my soul. Did you ever? Did you *ever* hear of a bird sleeping upside down before, ladies? Do you think she *was* asleep – or fainted?'

'I think she was asleep,' said Gertrude crossly. 'And I think it's a very stupid way to sleep. No wonder

83

she's so addle-witted. I wouldn't pay any more heed to her, Mr Mendelson.'

But still Mr Mendelson, who was very fond of little Sam, and wanted to keep his promise, continued to worry about Rosa, and to follow her about the park, anxiously begging her to come down out of tall trees and warning her against any large birds that chanced to fly past. And Rosa continued to take very little notice of anything that Mr Mendelson said. But she seemed quite fond of him in her feather-pated way, and spent at least an hour each day sitting on top of his head, cooing and chuckling to herself.

Naturally it was not long before the gipsy, Dan Sligo, noticed Rosa.

Dan Sligo had a hut in the woods outside Midnight Park, and made a living from picking things up cheap and selling them dear; he poached pheasants and snared rabbits and stole horses, which he dyed a different colour and sold back to their original masters. He was very interested in pigeons, too; he had one himself, called Cooey, who was a trained thief; Dan had taught her to fly in through open windows, pick up any small valuables that were lying about, and bring them back to him. The minute Dan laid eyes on Rosa, he wanted to know all about her.

''Day to 'ee, Mr Mendelson,' he said, one sunny morning, strolling up to where the old pony stood, watching Rosa take a bath in the pond, and calling anxious advice.

'Excuse me, Rosa, you are going in too deep! Come nearer to the edge, *please*! Who knows what lives in that pond? There might be a giant pike, that would gobble you up!'

'Rrrrrrrrkety splash,' replied Rosa, taking no notice whatsoever.

'Got a new friend then, Mr M?' inquired Dan Sligo, looking with admiration at Rosa's fat white chest and strawberry-ice-coloured eyes.

'Her name is Rosa. She does not belong to me,' said Mr Mendelson anxiously. 'She is little Sam's, and he has left her in my charge.'

'Very nice too,' said Dan Sligo. 'Very pretty turn of flight she has!' And he watched Rosa, who now, to dry herself off, suddenly rose up into the air, spraying pond-water in all directions, and then did a whole series of back-somersaults, going so fast that she looked like the tip of a fat white pencil drawing a long row of loops over the bright autumn sky.

'Ought to be in a circus, she did,' Dan Sligo said. 'Seems a shame she should just stay here in this ol' park, where there's no one to see her.'

'*I'm* here,' pointed out Mr Mendelson. '(Rosa! Please take *care*! You nearly hit the pine tree!)'

'That wasn't quite what I had in mind – meaning no disrespect,' said Dan Sligo. 'My meaning, see, is that a handsome liddle bird like that, so clever an' all, did oughta be doing her tricks in front o' crowned heads, not where there's only an old powny and a pair o' meddlesome mice as minds everyone's business but their own.'

Mr Mendelson did not answer. For one thing, he had no idea what Dan Sligo meant by crowned heads.

'Where does she sleep, then?' asked Dan Sligo idly. 'In the loft?'

'Oh, no,' Mr Mendelson said hastily. 'She sleeps out in the park – fresh air's better – sometimes in one place, sometimes another.'

He did not mention what a heavy sleeper Rosa was.

''Tis too sharp, now, nights, for a delicate-reared bird to be a-roosting out in the frizzling-cold air,' said Dan Sligo reprovingly. 'She could lodge wi' me, and welcome; there's Cooey's dovecote by my cabin – plenny o' room for two – she could bide there till young Master Sam do come home from school.'

'No, thank you,' said Mr Mendelson at once and very politely. 'Rosa is not fond of being shut up.'

'Folks bain't allus fond o' what's good for 'em,' said Dan Sligo with a wink. 'Suppose ol' Mars Fox do come along one night and take a fancy to carry 'er off? Then what'd 'ee say to liddle Sam when he come home from school?'

And he walked slowly off, leaving Mr Mendelson very worried.

'Suppose a fox *should* catch Rosa?' he said to Gertrude and Bertha next morning, when they were brushing his coat.

'Good riddance!' sniffed Bertha.

But Gertrude said,

'She can look after herself. She's big and fat enough, goodness knows!'

'Besides,' pointed out Bertha, 'she always hangs from quite a high branch when she's asleep in that crazy way of hers. No fox could jump up so high.'

Nevertheless, next day, Rosa was missing.

All day long Mr Mendelson wandered about the park, quite beside himself with worry, calling, 'Rosa! Rosa! Where are you? If you are hiding, come out, please, at once! This is quite important!' But there came no giggling coo from any of the trees he approached, and he saw no fat white fluttering form turning somersaults in the air.

'Do you think a fox did get her?' Mr Mendelson said miserably to the mice. 'Oh, how shall I ever be able to face little Sam?'

'If it had been a fox, there would be feathers,' said the knowledgeable Bertha. 'No, I think Dan Sligo came and grabbed her in the night. After all, he has tried to steal your piano – *and* your watch. We know he is a thief. You should have woken up, Mr Mendelson!'

'I get so tired, following Rosa all day long,' confessed

the old pony. 'What do you think we should do, Bertha?'

'We must go on a rescue expedition,' decided the mice. 'As soon as it is dark, Mr Mendelson, we must go to Dan Sligo's cabin. You have been there, you must show us the way.'

'Oy, my, shall I ever be able to find it in the dark?' he sighed. 'It is such a long time since little Sam and I used to go riding through those woods.'

That evening, instead of holding their usual six-o'clock concert of piano music, the two mice climbed up and found themselves comfortable seats in Mr Mendelson's thick mane, and he carried them to the north end of Midnight Park and out through the gateway into a piece of very thick and tangly woodland which was known as Pharaoh's Forest, because it belonged to nobody in particular and the gipsies had always camped in it.

Here Mr Mendelson and the mice would soon have been in difficulties, for he really had no notion which way to go, and the trees and bushes were so very close together. But fortunately Bertha and Gertrude were able to ask directions from their cousins the bats, who were busy flying to and fro in the dark scooping up night-flying insects, and the bats guided Mr Mendelson through the tangly wood until they came to Dan Sligo's cabin, which was very cunningly hidden in the most tangly part of all, a little sunken dell which had a thicket of yew and hawthorn bushes all round it, growing tight together, and divided by two little narrow paths leading through: one for Dan to go home by, and the second for him to leave by, very fast, if he saw visitors coming whom he did not wish to meet.

However, luckily, at this time of night Dan Sligo was always away from home, setting out paper bags filled with raisins and lined with treacle to catch pheasants,

and looking over his rabbit snares. Since the cabin was dark and silent Mr Mendelson was able to move softly out into the untidy patch of grass which lay between the cabin and the one-legged dovecote where Cooey the pigeon lived.

Standing underneath the dovecote Mr Mendelson raised his head and called softly,

'Rosa? Are you inside there?'

Dead silence from inside the dovecote.

'Oh my stars!' Mr Mendelson whispered to the mice. 'Suppose we were wrong? Suppose she's not there?'

'Don't forget what a heavy sleeper she is!' said Gertrude. 'Hold your head as high as you can, Mr Mendelson, and I'll run up your nose and see if I can jump on to the dovecote.'

The dovecote was not very high. Gertrude managed to do this.

'The door's tied shut with a piece of string!' she whispered. 'I shall have to gnaw through that.'

Then there was a silence, in which they could hear Gertrude's sharp teeth chewing away at the string, and a couple of owls calling in the distance.

Then – spang! – the string broke, and Gertrude edged open the door.

At this moment the moon drifted out from behind a cloud, and Gertrude, looking through the door into the dovecote, received the shock of her life.

'What's the matter?' whispered Mr Mendelson anxiously, seeing her stand open-mouthed.

'What's up, Gertrude?' called Bertha. 'Why are you gaping like a gudgeon? Isn't Rosa there?'

'Well –' said Gertrude slowly, 'there's two pigeons here, all right – fast asleep – and one of them is Dan Sligo's Cooey – but I don't think the other one can be Rosa.'

'Why not?'

'She's pink.'

'Rubbish!' said Bertha. 'You can't tell if she's pink in this light.'

'Yes I can,' said Gertrude.

'Well,' said Bertha, 'is she hanging upside down?'

'Yes, she is.'

'Then it's Rosa. No other pigeon in the whole *world* sleeps in that totty-headed manner. Wake her up!'

'Perhaps you're right,' said Gertrude.

'Of course I'm right! Do me a favour! Just get her out of there, before Dan Sligo comes back.'

So Gertrude climbed up inside the dovecote to the perch, and nipped the leg of the pink pigeon, who woke with a slow and sleepy crooning coo –

'Crrrrrroooo – ah!' that was halfway between a coo and a yawn.

'Come along out of there!' hissed Gertrude. 'We are rescuing you!'

'Hrrrrescuoooo – coo?'

'Oh, *come* on, Rosa!' shouted Bertha impatiently from the tip of Mr Mendelson's nose. 'Hurry up! We can't wait about here all night.'

At last Rosa came yawning out into the moonlight (Cooey, who was an even heavier sleeper, never woke at all). Gertrude pushed the dovecote door to again, Mr Mendelson reached up his nose once more, and Gertrude jumped and Rosa flopped down on to the crown of his head.

Just in time: for a bat whirled past at that moment shrilling out in a tiny voice.

'Pssst! Dan Sligo's coming back through the wood carrying two pheasants and a hare!'

Mr Mendelson slipped away as silently as he could along Dan Sligo's emergency escape-way, and the bats guided them back through Pharaoh's Forest as far as the entrance to Midnight Park. Here, out of the trees and into clear moonlight, they were able to see that Rosa was indeed a bright rose-colour.

'What *happened* to you?' said Mr Mendelson, aghast.

'Dan Sligo put me in a bath,' giggled Rosa.

'A *bath*? said Gertrude. 'It must have been a bath of pink paint.'

They were all quite tired, and fell asleep the moment they reached Mr Mendelson's oak, where the mice retired to their burrows.

Next morning, though, the mice came out early, to look at Rosa – who was a bright, bright pink – as pink as peonies, pink as sweet-peas, even pinker than raspberry icing. There she hung, pink all over, from the branch above their heads.

Mr Mendelson was very upset.

'I'm sure Sam won't want a pink pigeon! What ever is he going to say?'

'What's more to the point,' said Bertha, 'what will Dan Sligo do?'

Dan Sligo soon came hurrying across the park. He thought Rosa must somehow have opened the door herself and escaped.

'That's my Samoan tooth-billed pink Pigeon you've got there!' he said.

'Oh, no it isn't!' said Bertha. 'It's our Rosa. Anybody knows that she's the only pigeon in England who sleeps upside down.'

'Besides,' added Gertrude, 'she's wearing her leg-band – dyed pink – and it says ROSA – anybody can see that too.'

Dan Sligo was very annoyed that he had forgotten the leg-band.

'We had her coloured pink,' said Bertha sweetly. 'We thought little Sam would enjoy the colour.'

Rosa enjoyed it too. When she woke, she turned about a hundred back-somersaults, looking like a pink poppy that had gone mad in mid-air.

Dan Sligo stamped off, very angry indeed.

'I wouldn't try colouring Mr Mendelson pink!' shouted the mice after him. 'You'd need a bath as big as a pond!'

Mr Mendelson was still worried as to what little Sam would say when he came home. But luckily the colour faded very fast; rain and sun bleached it to pale pink –

much to Rosa's disgust; soon the dye had all washed off her feathers and by the time of Sam's return she was her fat white self again.

Mr Mendelson Learns to Fly

Spring had come back to Midnight Park. The hawthorn bushes were covered so thickly with white blossom that they looked like huge pale sea-urchins dotted about over the grass. The swallows were swooping and screaming, and old Mr Mendelson was watching them wistfully.

'Wouldn't you like to be able to do that?' he said to Bertha the fieldmouse, who was combing out his forelock with a thistle-head.

'Do me a favour!'

A swallow shot by them, faster than a rifle-bullet, and Bertha looked after it indignantly.

'Who wants to eat *flies*?' she said. 'Pushing past people in mid-air in that vulgar way, too! If you ask me, their parents never taught them manners!'

'But they are so quick and neat,' said Mr Mendelson enviously. 'I love to watch the tricks they play in the air. Oh, if only I could fly!'

'Mr *Mendelson*! Are you out of your *mind*? A *horse*, *flying*? Please! Next you'll be asking for fish on legs and mice in the sea. Things are in their proper places, and they should stay there.'

Mr Mendelson said no more to Bertha on the subject of flying, but he continued to watch the swallows with envy.

And he made up a little poem which he said to himself sometimes.

It went:

'I
Wish that I could fly.'

He did not say it aloud, for he feared the mice might laugh at him.

'It must be so cool, up there, shooting through the air as fast as that,' he thought.

In Midnight Park it was hot. Spring had turned to a dusty dry summer. The sheep in the park had nibbled the grass down until it was as smooth as a tablecloth. Not a whisper of breeze disturbed the leaves; even in the shade under Mr Mendelson's big oak tree the air was as warm and thick as rice-pudding. Mr Mendelson stood flicking away the flies with his tail and wishing for a cool wind – or a nice shower of rain – even a little hail or snow would make a pleasant change, he thought.

Then little Sam came home from school. That made a pleasant change, because Sam came and talked to Mr Mendelson under the oak, and brushed off the flies with a leafy bough, and he brought Mr Mendelson bits of carrot and juicy apples.

'Somebody ought to invent a fly-swatting machine,' he said to Mr Mendelson, fanning away. 'I will when I'm grown up.'

Then young Sam made friends with young Tim Lee, who was the son of old Tim Lee, the blacksmith. Both boys had rollerskates, and they used to practise skating in the park. Old Mr Mendelson enjoyed watching them almost as much as he enjoyed watching the swallows. At first they skated up and down the smooth track that had once led to the big house (now burned down). Then, as they grew more expert, and the grass grew shorter and dryer, they skated on the grass.

By this time Mr Mendelson thought they were quite as clever as the swallows; they could glide in a long curve, shoot forward fast, turn round sharply, dart off again, almost as if they were flying, and almost as fast.

He watched them all day long.

One very sultry afternoon the boys had skated until they were too hot to go on, and then they had taken off their skates and flung themselves down beside Mr Mendelson under the oak tree.

Mr Mendelson drooped down his big head and sniffed at the rollerskates (which had been made by Tim's father) lying on the grass.

'Would *you* like a pair, old feller?' asked Sam, waving away the flies with his oak bough. 'If you could only skate you needn't mind the flies – you'd be going so fast you'd leave them behind!'

'Well, why shouldn't he try?' said Tim.

'You mean – skate? Well – why *shouldn't* he? Hey!

That's a good idea. He could wear your skates on his front feet and mine on his hind feet. Would you like that, Mr Mendelson?'

Mr Mendelson's eyes shone at the thought of speeding along as fast as the swallows.

'Of *course* he wants to try!' said Tim. 'Here, lift up your hind hoof, Mr Mendelson, while I tie on this skate!'

In a few moments, all four skates were securely tied on his feet, and Mr Mendelson suddenly found that he was in a different world, where the ground kept sliding away from under him. He moved one of his forefeet – and it suddenly shot off, on a track of its own, as if it were not part of him; he started to go after it, but his hind feet had intentions of their own; one of them went backwards and the other went sideways. All of a sudden Mr Mendelson was flat on his barrel-stomach, with his legs each pointing a different way.

'Easy does it, old feller!' said little Sam. 'Now – *slowly*!' – when they had raised Mr Mendelson from the ground. 'Push with your hind feet – ah – not so hard!' – as Mr Mendelson struck out with both rear hoofs and almost catapulted himself into the trunk of a great chestnut tree. 'Gently – just one small push at a time.'

With a boy walking on each side and guiding him, Mr Mendelson started across the wide expanse of short grass. All the sheep stopped their nibbling and stared, not rudely, but with that look of stupid and rather superior astonishment that sheep wear when they see any new thing.

The two fieldmice, Bertha and Gertrude, came yawning out from their after-lunch nap in time to see Mr Mendelson glide carefully past. Sam had hold of his forelock, and Tim of his mane; which was just as well; for Mr Mendelson's feet were shooting out in all directions like billiard balls. But just at this moment he was managing to stay upright and keep moving in one direction; although he looked nervous, he also looked very excited and proud of himself.

Not every Orkney pony, after all, learns to skate after the age of twenty.

'*Mr Mendelson!*' exclaimed Bertha, quite scandalized. 'What *do* you think you are doing?'

'I'm learning to fly – I mean, skate,' he panted, as he shot past her. Both boys were having to trot quite fast, now, to keep up with him. And his speed was increasing.

'Are you crazy?' Gertrude shouted after him. 'You will have a terrible accident. You'll probably break

your neck – you'll run into a tree! Will you look at that old idiot,' she said to her sister, 'careering along as if he had entered for the Derby! Mr Mendelson! Come back! You'll be killed – sure as eggs is eggs!'

These shouts of warning went unheard by Mr Mendelson, who was now a long way down the park, going faster and faster. It was not that he was skating better – simply that he had to go very fast in order to keep up with his legs. And his legs were quite out of control, they seemed like the legs of some other pony.

'Stop him! Stop him!' shouted Tim and Sam, who had now been obliged to drop behind, for they could no longer keep up with Mr Mendelson's headlong pace.

They were shouting to the sheep, hoping the flock would bunch itself in front of Mr Mendelson and block his way – but instead, the sheep all scattered out of his way with loud cries of alarm.

'Baa-aaa-aaa! Miii-iii-ind ou-ou-ou-ou-out!'

The only person who took any notice of the boys' warning shouts was the gipsy, Dan Sligo, who always kept an ear open for any excitement in the park. He had heard the commotion, and now came to see what was going on.

Even he was startled at the sight of Mr Mendelson, streaking across the grass in his direction like a small black furry rocket.

'What the dickens have got into the old powny, then?' he exclaimed in wonder. 'I never did see 'im goo so faaaarst before, not in all my live-a-long days! Did he get bitten by one o' they garble-flies?' Then he saw the rollerskates on Mr Mendelson's hoofs, and began to understand the situation.

'Pity there bain't a haystack in's way – that'd act as a buffer and stop the owd feller,' Dan Sligo said thoughtfully.

But there was not a haystack. The hay had all been cut and carted into a barn; the men had been at work

two days before with hay-bogies, which are flat plat-
forms on wheels. One of the bogies was still standing
out on the grass, and Dan, observing it, was struck with
an idea. Mr Mendelson was coming in his direction.
Dan pushed the bogie rapidly so that it stood in Mr
Mendelson's way, and then he turned it and tilted it,
so that its front edge rested on the ground, sloping down
towards Mr Mendelson. Hay-bogies are made to tilt in
this way, so that large haycocks can be hauled straight
on to them off the ground, all in one pile.

Now, in tilting the hay-bogie down towards the on-
coming Mr Mendelson, Dan Sligo thought he would be

able to stop the old pony. He thought that either Mr Mendelson would start up the slope, and lose speed, and slide back down again; or, possibly, that he would skate right up to the top of the slope, and drop off and come to a stop on the ground the other side.

But what actually happened was that Mr Mendelson shot up the slope of the bogie, and then catapulted straight on into the air, travelling onwards and upwards in the same line.

'Oy, mercy, I'm flying!' exclaimed Mr Mendelson. He had been silent with wonder and excitement all the time he had been speeding along the ground, but this was a bit more than he had bargained for.

'Saints save us!' muttered Dan Sligo the gipsy. ''Tis the very first time I ever did see a flying powny, and I'm rale sorry my old grandma bain't here to see the sight too.'

'Oh, Mr Mendelson!' cried little Sam racing up, quite out of breath, 'Please take care!'

'He'll be killed! He's sure to be killed!' lamented the mice, who had come scampering over the short grass, absolutely distracted with alarm.

'He must be ma-aaa-aaa-aaad!' remarked the sheep, all standing with their heads up and their eyes popping.

The Old Lord had come rolling out of the stable, where he lived, in his wheelchair, at the sound of all the uproar. He arrived just in time to see Mr Mendelson take off.

'*What* is that pony doing up there?' he inquired, very disapprovingly indeed, as Mr Mendelson reached the highest point of his flight. For a moment it looked as if the old pony would shoot right out of the park; but he was caught in the top of an ancient, thick, yew-and-holly hedge, which formed the boundary of the park on that side. There Mr Mendelson came to a stop; nothing could be seen of him but his head, sticking out of the top of the hedge, and his hind feet, sticking out of the side.

'Is this *your* doing, Dan Sligo?' said the Old Lord, looking up at the hind feet.

'As heaven's my witness, your honour, would I be doing a thing like that to the poor old powny?' said Dan virtuously.

'Very likely! You nearly always *do* seem to have a hand in such disgraceful occurrences!'

'Cross me heart, your worship, I had no part in it at

all, only to wheel the bogie in the way –' Dan Sligo was beginning, when Tim and Sam rushed up, and Sam said,

'It was us, grandfather – we tied the rollerskates on his feet – and I'm as sorry as can be –'

'Well, if it was you, you can get him down, and be quick about it!' said the Old Lord indignantly. 'What do you think he can be feeling, stuck up there in a holly tree?'

Dan Sligo goodnaturedly helped the boys fetch ladders and ropes, and tie a strap round Mr Mendelson's middle, and carefully lower him to the ground. It was a long and awkward job.

Dan took the precaution of removing the rollerskates from the old pony's hoofs before they began rescuing him – and it was not until next day that the boys realized they had not got their skates back. Dan Sligo had gone off with them.

Next time they met Dan he said, 'Well, I declare! If I haven't been and forgotten your skates again. There they lays at home. I'll be bringing 'em along,

s'arternoon, or tomorrow morning at latest –' But somehow he always forgot to bring them, and the boys never
saw those skates again.

As for Mr Mendelson, he was quite stiff for some
days, and rather silent. The mice had a long job getting
all the holly prickles out of his thick black fur coat, and
they scolded him all the time they were doing it.

'Careering about on rollerskates! Flying up into the

air! What *do* you think you are? A horse of your age!
Perching in a hedge! As if you were a bird! What next?'

Mr Mendelson listened to their scoldings in patient
silence. He had enjoyed the flight while it lasted – he

was glad he had done it – but he did not want to do it
again. The after-effects were not very enjoyable. He
made up another little poem, and said it to himself as
the mice brushed and combed and tut-tutted:

> 'Flying
> Is rather trying.'

Some other Young Puffins

THE WORST WITCH STRIKES AGAIN
Jill Murphy

Enid Nightshade, the new pupil at Miss Cackle's academy for witches, is not such a good influence on disaster-prone Mildred Hubble as their headmistress fondly imagined.

STORIES FOR UNDER-FIVES
STORIES FOR FIVE-YEAR-OLDS
STORIES FOR SIX-YEAR-OLDS
STORIES FOR SEVEN-YEAR-OLDS
STORIES FOR EIGHT-YEAR-OLDS
STORIES FOR NINE-YEAR-OLDS
Sara and Stephen Corrin

Well-chosen collections of superb stories, which have been carefully graded to suit the developing interests and imaginations of different age groups.

ALBERT ON THE FARM
ALBERT
ALBERT'S CHRISTMAS
Alison Jezard

Albert is a lively and lovable bear – whatever he and his friends are up to always turns into an uproarious adventure.

TWO VILLAGE DINOSAURS
Phyllis Arkle

Two dinosaurs spell double trouble as Dino and Sauro trample their amiable way through the village, causing chaos and confusion on every side.

DINNER AT ALBERTA'S
Russell Hoban

Arthur the crocodile has extremely bad manners
– until he is invited to Alberta's for dinner.

THE NEW RED BIKE
Simon Watson

Sixteen short stories about a lively and logical small
boy called Wallace, his nice parents, his daily
adventures and occasional disgraces, all told with
humour and understanding.

HIDE TILL DAYTIME
Joan Phipson

The two children had been locked into the big
department store by mistake at closing time, and
whose were those prowling steps they could hear
through the dark?

THE ADVENTURES OF SAM PIG
YOURS EVER, SAM PIG
SAM PIG GOES TO THE SEASIDE
SAM PIG GOES TO MARKET
SAM PIG AND SALLY
Alison Uttley

Collections of stories about Alison Uttley's best-loved
creation, Sam Pig, and his farm animal friends.

THE DIAL-A-STORY BOOK
H. E. Todd

Magic pops up in the strangest places when Bobby
and Barbara Brewster are around! A collection of
three-minute stories, specially written for the
GPO's Bedtime Story service.